Melody, the Music Queen

Written by: Jennifer Morgan, Ph.D

Illustrated by: Ananta Mohanta

Author's Note

It is normal to feel fear and worry sometimes. However, when these feelings prevent a child from doing or enjoying life activities, it is a bigger problem that cannot be ignored. Melody, the Music Queen, is a wonderful resource for introducing children to simple coping strategies for anxiety and building confidence. This is the second book of the C4 Collection book series that is meant to help promote and support children's mental health.

ISBN: 979-8-9854261-4-4

This Book Belongs To:

____

Word Scavenger Hunt

Can you find these underlined words in the book?

- <u>Anxiety</u> – An extreme feeling of worry and/or fear.

- <u>Coping</u> – Something a person does or thinks about to decrease stress or a negative emotion.

- <u>Counseling</u> – A safe place for a person to express different emotions and resolve a problem with help of a counselor.

- <u>Counselor</u> – A person who is trained to give advice and help people resolve problems.

- <u>Deep Breathing</u> – A relaxation skill that helps calm the body when feeling anxious or stressed.

  ➤ Let's practice! For 2 minutes, place one hand on your belly and one hand on your chest. Slowly breathe in through your nose (silently count to 5); then slowly breathe out through your mouth (for 5 counts). Good job! Make deep breathing fun by practicing with bubbles, a pinwheel, or dandelion!

- <u>Optimistic Talking</u> – Positive self-talk that makes a person feel hopeful about themselves or a situation.

- <u>Seeing the Positives</u> – Imagining good things that can happen in the moment or the future.

- <u>Stress</u> – A feeling of not being able to cope with a problem.

Hi, my name is Melody, and I call myself the music queen.

I like to dance, play instruments, and wear a sparkling crown when I sing.

In class, I daydream and wonder if I can perform at my school's talent show this year.

But I have one big problem, I can't sing in front of people because of my anxiety and fear.

"M ELODYYYY," called my teacher. "Are you working or daydreaming again?" "Oh, I'm working!" I answered. "Just thinking about my answer for question number 10."

With an awkward smile, I slouched in my chair to try and disappear. I felt controlled like a puppet and anxiety was my puppeteer.

You see, anxiety is a feeling of worry that something might go wrong. I feel this way while sitting in class or when I am on a stage singing a song.

My anxiety started in the 2nd grade, one night at my school's Christmas play. I stood on stage to sing my lines but nervously forgot what to say.

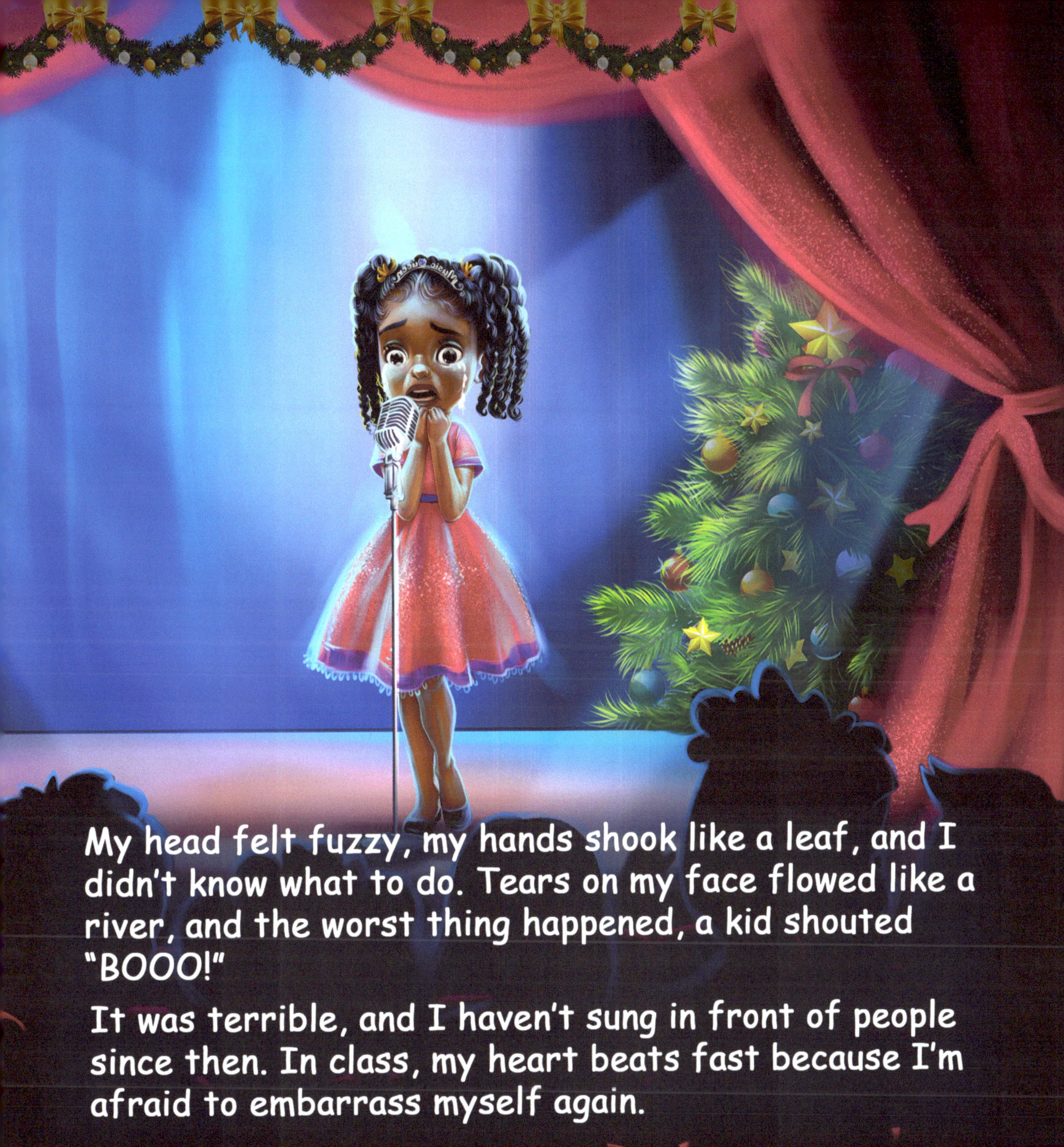

My head felt fuzzy, my hands shook like a leaf, and I didn't know what to do. Tears on my face flowed like a river, and the worst thing happened, a kid shouted "BOOO!"

It was terrible, and I haven't sung in front of people since then. In class, my heart beats fast because I'm afraid to embarrass myself again.

But I'm almost a fourth grader, and I want to be brave and not be worried anymore. If I lower my anxiety, I'll perform at the talent show and relax at school evermore.

RIIIING!

Well, that's the lunch bell, and I'm meeting with my best friend, KJ. I'll talk to him about my worries and some ideas to make them go away.

At lunch, KJ told me that he shares his worries with an adult he trusts. Ms. Riley, our school counselor, is helpful so we thought meeting with her was a must!

Do
Not
Waste
food

After lunch, I met with Ms. Riley and agreed to do counseling with her every week. She taught me strategies to lower my anxiety, including the "S.T.O.P." technique.

Ms. Riley said with a smile, "each letter in the word S.T.O.P. is a strategy you should know. If you practice them every day, you will lower your anxiety and perhaps sing at the talent show."

"Really?" I said with surprise. "Sounds great, let's go!" So, Ms. Riley described each strategy, starting with the letter S.

S

"**S**" is for *See the Positives* by imagining what will go right.

T

"T" is for **Take Deep Breaths** to relax your body if you're feeling fright.

"O" is for **Optimistic Talking** when you feel nervous or scared. For example, you can say "I got this!" or "don't worry, I'm prepared."

P

"**P**" is for ***Practice Facing Your Fear Every day.*** You'll practice singing in front of friends until your anxiety lowers or goes away.

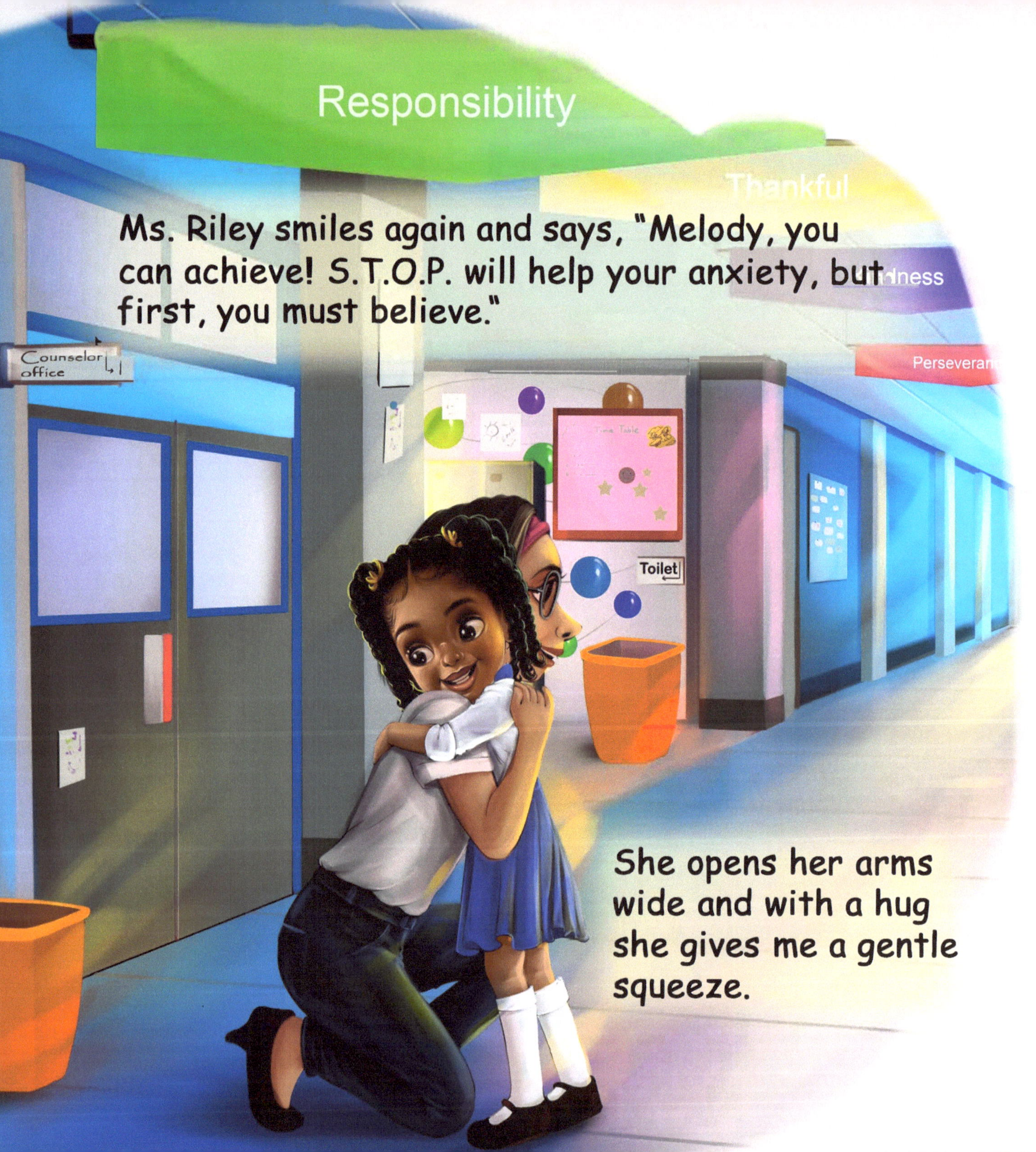

Ms. Riley smiles again and says, "Melody, you can achieve! S.T.O.P. will help your anxiety, but first, you must believe."

She opens her arms wide and with a hug she gives me a gentle squeeze.

For the next four weeks, I practiced S.T.O.P. with my mom and best friend. I practiced at home and school with hopes that my problem with anxiety would end.

On talent show night, I felt a little fright but not as much as before. The strategies of S.T.O.P. helped me a lot, and I was ready to perform once more.

I imagined my success by performing my best, exactly how I practiced. I took deep breaths to lower my stress and muttered, "Melody, you got this!"

In a matter of seconds, I heard a cheer, and my name was called aloud. It was my turn to stand on stage and face the rowdy crowd.

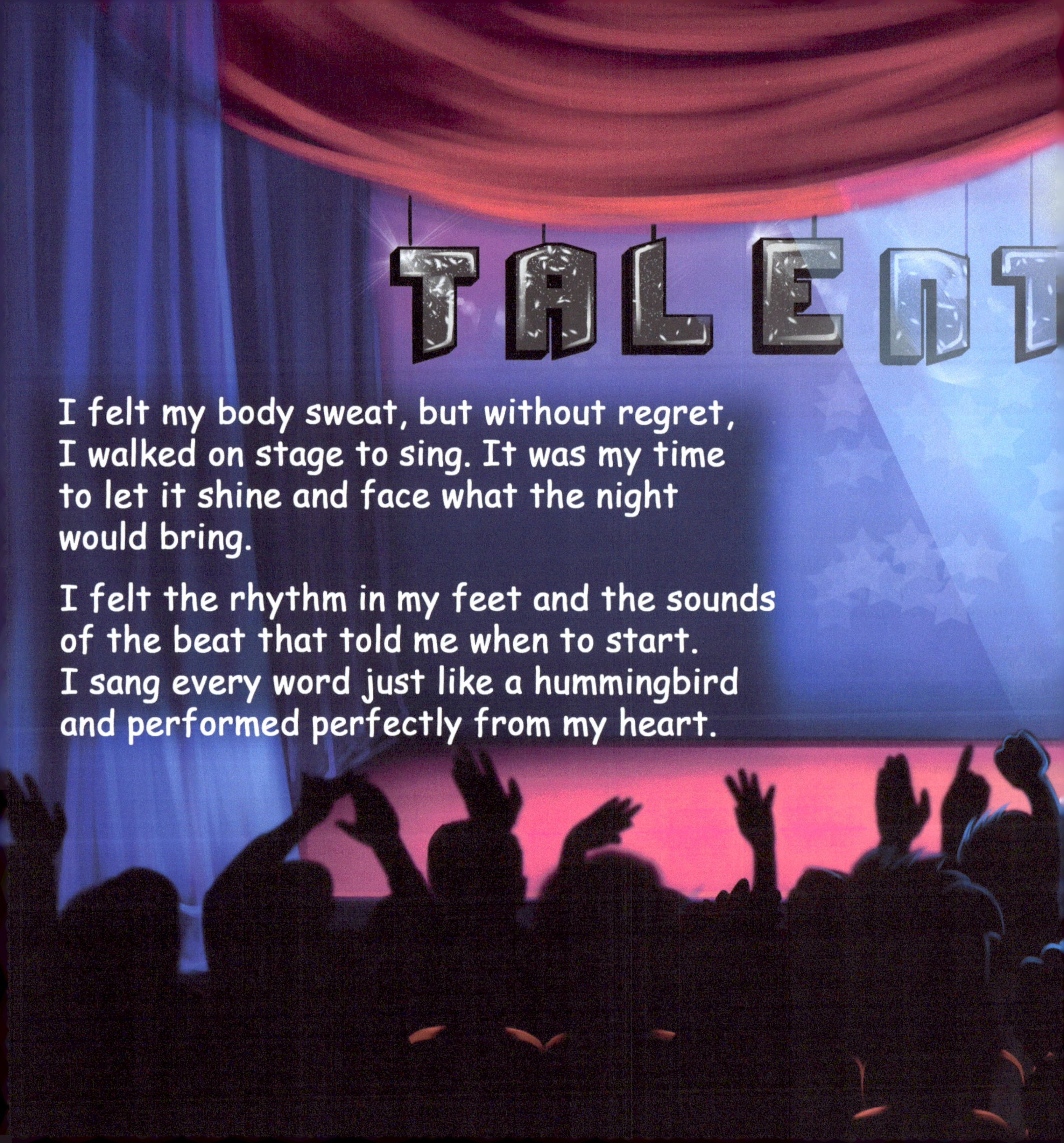

TALENT

I felt my body sweat, but without regret,
I walked on stage to sing. It was my time
to let it shine and face what the night
would bring.

I felt the rhythm in my feet and the sounds
of the beat that told me when to start.
I sang every word just like a hummingbird
and performed perfectly from my heart.

I grooved to the left, then grooved to the right; I had so much fun with my song. To my surprise, I impressed the crowd and could hear people singing along!

Mel-o-dy! Mel-o-dy! The crowd cheered my name. I enjoyed every second of my performance without feeling any shame.

Wow! I thought. What a rush of joy to finally face my fear! I ran to my mom with a smile on my face that ran from ear to ear.

Never again, will anxiety win because I will control the things I do. I am a music queen who is proud to be seen, and with S.T.O.P. anyone can achieve too.

Music Queen